GUESS WHAT?

BY

JOAN K. ASANTE

First published in the United Kingdom
Imprint: Independent Publishing Network
Artwork by Joan K. Asante and Unicorn Productions
Edited by: Joan K. Asante
ISBN: 978-1-80068-947-3

To all children
who deserve to see themselves
in the best way

HI! I'm Jaz, today is a great day!
Me and my family are out in the park.
I love playing in the park.

My favourite is the the swing
My friends call me "Jaz the champ"
because of how high I go,

I swing so high, past the sky,

I have balloons, one for me and one for my baby sister Naya.

She doesn't hold it properly, she **always** holds her dummy

but I have an idea....

Look! The dummy is flying too high up I can't get it!
Looks like it's on its way to space!

"Jaz! It's time to go" shouts Mum

It's time for bed now.
But I know Naya won't sleep
without her dummy.

Ready, Set....

GUESS WHAT?

The first rockets were invented about 800 years ago and were used for fireworks.

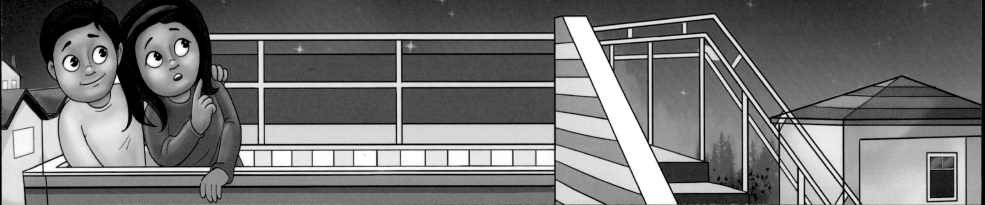

GUESS WHAT?

Fun Fact:
Did you know the moon
was once a piece of the Earth?

Space is Amazing!

Now time to look out for the

balloon with the dummy

"Oh look I think I've found it.
Over there."

What an adventure! Now it's time to get home.

Goodnight Galaxy. Our mission is complete.

References

Smithsonian National Air and Space Musuem
https://airandspace.si.edu/stories/editorial/first-fireworks-origins-rocket

Lego.com
https://www.lego.com/en-sg/kids/articles/city/blast-off-with-fun-rocket-facts

NASA -Goddard Flight Center
https://asd.gsfc.nasa.gov/blueshift/index.php/2015/07/22/
how-many-stars-in-the-milky-way/

NASA
https://www.nasa.gov/topics/universe/features/universe20110722.html

National Geographic
https://www.nationalgeographic.com/science/article/150713
-pluto-flyby-ten-questions-answered-space

Natural History Museum
https://www.nhm.ac.uk/discover/how-did-the-moon-form.html#:~:text=Earth's%
20greatest%20spinoff&text=The%20giant%2Dimpact%20model%20suggests,
Moon%20as%20we%20know%20it.